THE HEDGEHOG'S BALLOON

NICK BUTTERWORTH

TED SMART

Percy the park keeper looked up from
his work and gazed in wonder.
"Two red ones. . . a blue one. . . there's
a yellow one. . . and another blue one. . ."

Percy was counting balloons.
"I wonder where they're
coming from," he said to himself.
"Somebody must have had a party."
He put down his trowel and wiped
his hands.
"Well, if nobody wants them," he said,
"I think I'll help myself."

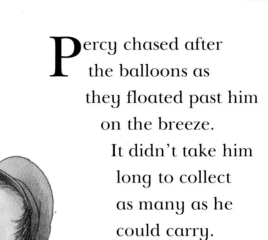

Percy chased after
the balloons as
they floated past him
on the breeze.
It didn't take him
long to collect
as many as he
could carry.
He began
to walk back
towards his
hut, whistling
happily.

Suddenly, Percy stopped. He could hear a faint sound coming from a tree stump nearby. It was not a happy sound.

"Someone's crying," said Percy. "Oh dear." He let go of his balloons and hurried over to the stump.

Sitting on the tree stump, and looking
very upset, was a hedgehog. Two mice
were doing their best to comfort him.

"Goodness me," said Percy. "Whatever
is the matter?"

"It's all these balloons," said the hedgehog.

Then, in between sniffs and sobs, he explained to Percy how he had always loved balloons. The trouble was that he could never have them because they would always burst on his spines.

"It's just not fair!" And the hedgehog burst into tears again.

"You poor thing," said Percy. He tried to put his arm around the hedgehog but took it away at once.

"Ouch," he said.

Then Percy took one of his thick gardening gloves out of his pocket and put it on. The hedgehog nestled into his hand.

"I think everyone should be able to play
with balloons," said Percy. "And that
includes hedgehogs."

He put on the other glove and gently
carried the hedgehog towards an old store
shed. The two mice followed.

The mice watched Percy through the window. He set the hedgehog down on a workbench and then he took a tin from a shelf. He opened the lid.

"What's Percy doing?" said one of the mice. "What's in that box?"

"I don't know," said the other mouse. "I can't see properly."

The mice didn't have to wait long to find out. Percy picked up the hedgehog and brought him outside.

"There!" said Percy. "A good idea, even if I say so myself! I think those balloons will be safe now."

The mice clapped and the hedgehog beamed. He thought how smart he must look, wearing his corks.

Percy caught hold of a bright yellow
balloon.

"Here you are," said Percy as he
handed it to the hedgehog. "Your very
first balloon."

The hedgehog took the balloon and
with a great big smile on his face,
he scampered off with the balloon floating
beside him.

"Another satisfied customer," said
Percy, feeling pleased with himself.

P ercy turned to go back to his hut. But suddenly, there came a loud BANG!

"Oops!" said Percy. "One of the corks must have come off. It's a good job we've got plenty of balloons!"

"Don't worry," Percy called to the hedgehog, "I'm coming. . ."

Nick Butterworth

Nick Butterworth was born in North
London in 1946 and grew up in a
sweet shop in Essex. He now lives
in Suffolk with his wife Annette
and their two children,
Ben and Amanda.

The inspiration for the Percy the Park Keeper
books came from Nick Butterworth's many walks
through the local park with the family dog, Jake.
The stories have sold nearly two million copies
and are loved by children all around the world.